Life's Too Short
Not to Live It
As a Texan

By Peg Hein

Illustrations by Kathryn Lewis

Published by Kathryn Designs, Austin, TX

Life's Too Short Not to Live It as a Texan
By Peg Hein

Cover design and illustrations: Kathryn Lewis
Editor and interior design: Peter Lewis

Published by Kathryn Designs
13 Sundown Parkway
Austin, Texas 78746
(512) 328-5042

ISBN 0-9628815-0-3
0 9 8 7 6 5 4 3 2 1
Printed and bound in the State of Texas, United States of America

TO MARV, NICK AND LAURA
OUR SPECIAL NATURALIZED TEXANS

AND TO PETE, WHO DEMONSTRATED TRUE TEXAS
COURAGE BY EDITING HIS MOTHER-IN-LAW'S WORDS
AND HIS WIFE'S ART

Contents

Introduction

Life's too short not to live it as a Texan. Being Texan is a state of mind arising from the history, heroes, legends, people, places and attitudes of this richly diverse land.

If you're a newcomer to the state, we hope this book will help get you started thinking in the Texas state of mind. Before too long you'll be able to think of your own reasons why Texas is such a special place.

If you're a visitor, we hope this book will accompany you home, to remind you of the wonderful times you had here. Because being Texan is a state of mind, you may discover that you can live life as a Texan even if you're far away.

If you've never been to Texas, this book is a sampler of what you're missing.

And if you're a Lone Star native, this book is full of affirmations. Perhaps we can come closer to discovering, in the following pages, just what it means to be Texan.

Peg Hein
September 1991

Here's What They Say About Texas

"Other states were carved or born, Texas grew from hide and horn."
Anonymous

"The province of Texas will be the richest state in our union, without any exception." - Thomas Jefferson

"Texas is a state of mind. Texas is an obsession. Above all, Texas is a nation in every sense of the word."- John Steinbeck.

"You-all can go to Hell; I'm a-goin to Texas." - Davy Crockett, after voters in Tennessee declined to re-elect him to Congress.

If I owned Texas and Hell, I'd rent out Texas and live in Hell."
- Gen. Philip Sheridan, after being stationed at a frontier fort
 in West Texas.

"I must say as to what I have seen of Texas, it is the garden spot of the world. The best land and the best prospects for health I ever saw, and I do believe it is a fortune for any man to come here. There is a world of country here to settle."
- Davy Crockett

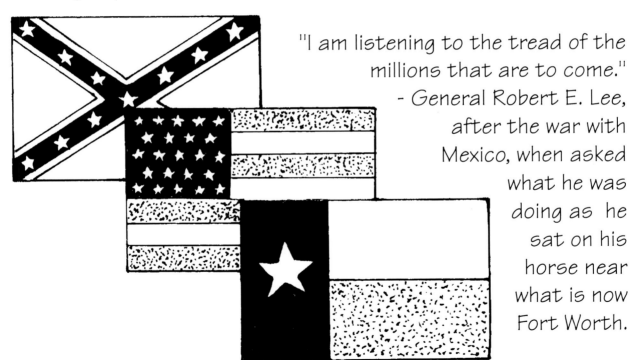

"I am listening to the tread of the millions that are to come."
- General Robert E. Lee, after the war with Mexico, when asked what he was doing as he sat on his horse near what is now Fort Worth.

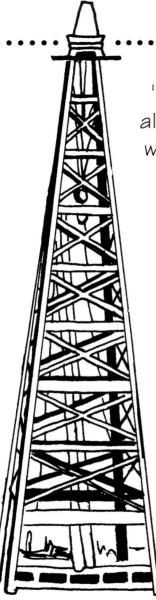

"Texas is my mistress, and to her I am devoting all my my time and affection. When I get through with my duties to her, then I may marry, but not before." - Stephen F. Austin, asked why he had never married.

"Damn it, cattle can't drink that stuff." - W.T. Waggoner in 1911, before he realized that the oil oozing from the ground on his ranch might actually be worth something. It made him very rich.

"There's nothing to see in East Texas . . . there's too many trees in the way." - a West Texan's observance

"Texas is a blend of valor and swagger." - Carl Sandburg

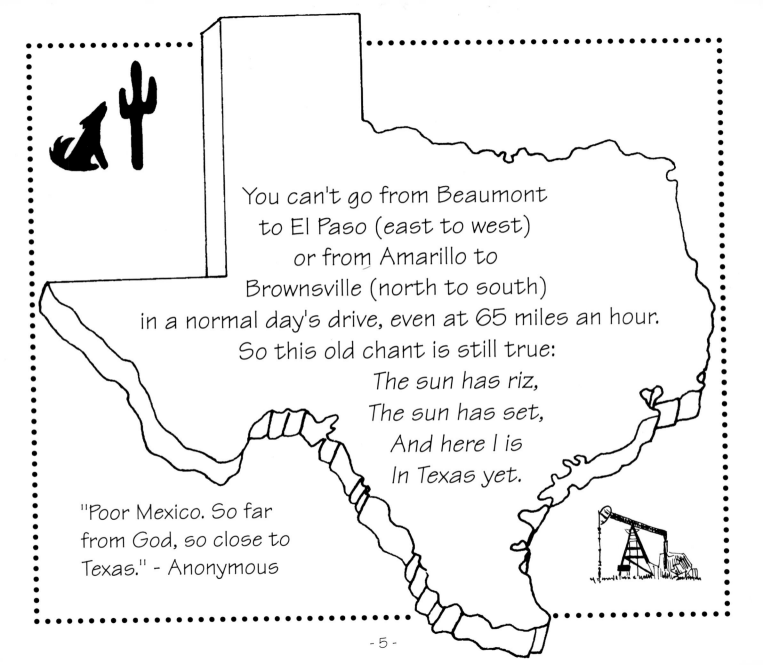

You can't go from Beaumont
to El Paso (east to west)
or from Amarillo to
Brownsville (north to south)
in a normal day's drive, even at 65 miles an hour.
So this old chant is still true:
The sun has riz,
The sun has set,
And here I is
In Texas yet.

"Poor Mexico. So far
from God, so close to
Texas." - Anonymous

"It's a deceitful country -- hard, mean -- with floods and droughts and tornadoes. But look at it, God almighty, it's so beautiful." - An old Texas rancher, when asked what he thought of Texas.

"Oh, how I wish I had the power to describe the wonderful country as I saw it then." - James B. Gillett, Texas Ranger

"Texans always move them." - General Lee, at the Battle of the Wilderness in the War of Northern Aggression, when he heard of the success of a Texas company after others failed.

"Mein Gott, vot a country dis Texas iss."
- German settler

"I am forced to conclude that God made Texas on his day off, for pure entertainment, just to prove what diversity could be crammed into one section of earth by a really top hand." - Mary Lasswell

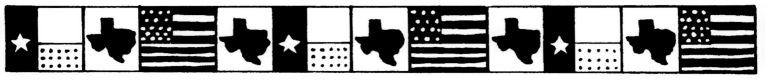

About half of the people now living in Texas migrated here within the last 30 years. Many of them have moments when they wonder if they can be called "Texans" yet. Here are some guidelines:

You Know You're A Texan . . .

. . . When you realize that the jalapeños on your nachos no longer make the tears run down your cheeks, or make you gasp for water.

. . . When you are waiting to eat at a restaurant outside Texas and wonder where the salsa and tortilla chips are.

. . . When you know what a kicker is.

. . . When you realize that only damn fools or Yankees try to predict Texas weather.

. . . When you realize that at least half of your friends drive either pickups or Suburbans.

. . . When you know that the Red River War refers to the Oklahoma-Texas football game played in Dallas.

. . . When you automatically stand up as the band starts to play "I've Been Working On The Railroad."

. . . When you have more than one friend named Bubba.

. . . When you start to squeeze three syllables out of words that you know have only two. Like Tay-ik-suss.

. . . When you're more comfortable in boots than you are in topsiders.

. . . When you wonder for the first time whether you can get away with wearing boots with a business suit.

. . . When you hear yourself saying, "I was just fixin' to do that," and it doesn't sound funny.

. . . When you say "y'all" instead of "you guys."

. . . When you catch yourself saying, "George Bush isn't really a Texan."

. . . When you learn the Texas Two-Step and the Cotton-Eyed Joe.

. . . When you no longer flinch at the sight of lizards or cockroaches the size of mice.

. . . When you tell Aggie jokes, even though you know how smart the Texas A&M people really are.

. . . When you have at least one radio button in your car tuned to a country music station, or at least one Willie Nelson tape on the dash.

. . . When you think, "Why go to New York when we have the Houston Opera here?"

my heart is broke and so is my truck
my wife's run off 'n I'm down on my luck...
think I'll have a beer

. . . When you can't remember the new name of your bank.

. . . When the thought of living anywhere else makes you sad.

.. . . When you know that all those little lakes in the ranch country are called tanks, and are really watering holes for sheep and cattle.

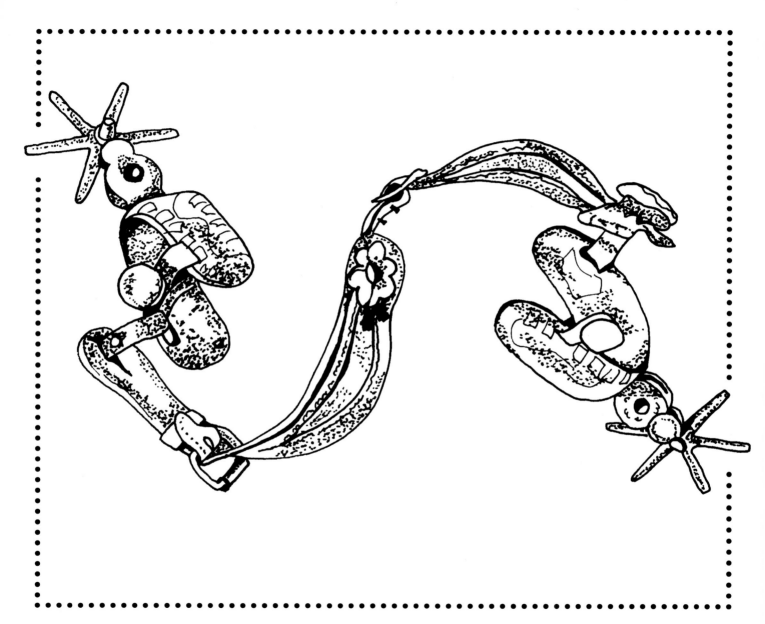

Texas Rangers

Texas Rangers were the only law in Texas for many years. Although there were never more than 500 Rangers at a time, they were expected to protect Texas settlers in west and south Texas from hostile Indians, Mexicans, murderers, cattle rustlers and horse thieves. The badly outnumbered Rangers were sometimes accused of "shooting first and asking questions later." Their territory was vast, their job was dangerous, and their pay was low.

To be a Texas Ranger, it was said, one had to
"ride like a Mexican,
track like a Comanche,
shoot like a Kentuckian,
and fight like the Devil."

The legendary Ranger
Capt. Bill McDonald said,
"No man that's in the wrong can stand up against
a fellow that's in the right and keeps a-comin."

Of Captain McDonald it was said: "He would charge
Hell single-handed with a bucket of water."

Sam Houston said, "You may withdraw every
regular soldier . . . from the border of Texas . . .
if you will give her but a single
regiment . . . of Texas Rangers."

Walter Prescott Webb, in the finest account written about the Rangers, said: "Surely enough has been written about men who swagger, fan hammers, and make hip shots. No Texas Ranger ever fanned a hammer when he was serious, or made a hip shot if he had time to catch a sight. The real Ranger has been a very quiet, deliberate, gentle person who could gaze calmly into the eye of a murderer, divine his thought, and anticipate his action; a man who could ride straight up to death."

The historian T.R. Fehrenbach wrote: "Rangers, born of the frontier, embodied many of the bedrock values of the frontier. They were brutal to enemies, loyal to friends, courteous to women, kind to old ladies."

One of the oldest and most often told Ranger stories is about the town besieged by a vicious mob. The Mayor sent for the Texas Rangers, but was distraught when a solitary Ranger got off the next train. The Ranger's response: "Well, you only got one riot, don't you?"

Stephen F. Austin employed the first Rangers as early as 1823. Today, Texas Rangers are still involved in law enforcement, but as a division of the State Department of Public Safety.

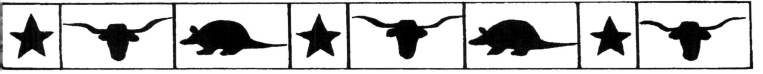

Texas Critters

Armadillos ("Texas Speed Bumps")

Poor, dead 'dillos, their feet pointing skyward, are the unofficial roadside decoration of Texas. When frightened, an armadillo will jump straight up into the air ... sometimes as high as four feet, but more often just to bumper level. Early Spaniards in Texas named it "little armored one," but scientists call it *Dasypus novemcinctus*, for its nine-banded shell. Blessed by neither speed nor brains nor good eyesight, the dillo's best defense is to roll into a ball and play dead. Dillos are also called Texas submarines because they walk across streams.

Horned Frog ("Horny Toad")

It's neither a frog nor a toad, but a lizard. The horny toad's scaly armor, hornlike spines and habit of spurting blood from its eye sockets when threatened causes some consternation upon first acquaintance, but it's really a delightful little critter to have in the garden, since it eats insects. Texas Christian University named its sports teams the Horned Frogs. The most famous Texas horny toad is Old Rip, who was found alive after being entombed 31 years in the cornerstone of the Eastland County Courthouse. He was immortalized in "Ripley's Believe It Or Not" and went on tour, drawing huge crowds.

Chaparrals ("Road Runners")

It's a bird that would rather run than fly. Road runners can achieve speeds of 15 mph and seem to enjoy drag-racing automobiles. They also enjoy preening from a perch atop rocks or stumps, where they can watch for tasty bugs, mice, scorpions and young snakes. Contrary to the cartoons, "beep beep" is not in its vocabulary.

Turkey Vultures ("Buzzards")

These critters win no prizes for beauty. Buzzards circling are a sign that some living creature below is seriously injured or dead, making them an unwelcome omen. On the positive side, these scavengers keep Texas free of animal carcasses.

Camels

Yes, camels. They were brought to Texas in the 1850's to be used as military pack animals between San Antonio and El Paso, and proved better than mules because they could travel many miles without food or water. They fell out of favor with Texans because of their surly dispositions and nasty habits (they spit on people). It seems unlikely that descendents of those early beasts survive today, but every now and then a traveler reports seeing a camel in the Big Bend area of West Texas.

Coyotes

Coyotes, cowboys and the lone prairie are part of the lore that makes up the myth of Texas. Their long, drawn-out howl sounds both threatening and forlorn. The coyote's habit of running with its tail between its legs makes people think it is cowardly.

The Texas Longhorn

These smart, tough and rangy beasts were so well suited for Texas that they became the foundation for most of the great ranches. Millions of longhorns were driven up the trails to the nearest railroad, where they were sometimes worth as little as a dollar a head. When railroads and barbed wire came to Texas, ranchers switched to heavier cattle that brought higher prices and produced better steaks. The longhorn was soon threatened with extinction. In recent years ranchers have discovered that breeding some longhorn blood into their purebreds results in animals that are hardier and more resistant to disease. Cowboys feared the longhorn, whose sharp horns can span eight feet from tip to tip, but they loved its rugged, independent and sometimes ornery spirit, too. If there is one animal that is recognized as a symbol of Texas (as well as of the University of Texas), it is the longhorn.

Africanized Honeybees ("Killer Bees")

Killer bees are newcomers to the list of Texas critters, but we've known they were coming for years. There have been more border guards watching for them than there are watching for drugs or illegal aliens! Killer bees are regular honeybees with an attitude problem. They are highly aggressive and swarm on their victims, but usually only after they have been provoked.

Fire Ants

The fire ant is the reason you rarely see a Texan walking barefoot or enjoying a picnic in the grass. Ounce for ounce these critters have more sting than any other varmint. (Most people think they bite, and they do, but just to hold their place while they bury their stingers in your hide.) They live up to their Latin name, Invictus (invincible), resisting all attempts to kill them. They are attracted to electricity, and most air conditioner and traffic light failures in Texas are caused by fire ant infestations.

Rattlesnakes

There has been some talk of listing the rattlesnake as an endangered species, because the good ol' boys at the rattlesnake roundups each spring say they are having a tougher time finding enough victims to make hatbands. The western diamondback is the most common species in Texas, and although they are said to be very shy critters, few people are interested in getting to know them well enough to verify it.

Jackrabbits

Their huge ears and powerful hind legs make jackrabbits easily distinguishable from the bunnies seen in other states. They run so fast it takes two people to see them, one to yell "Here they come!" and one to yell "There they go!" Jackrabbits are more common than jackalopes, which were the result of crossbreeding a jackrabbit and a whitetailed deer in an errant experiment by the Aggies at A&M.

Talkin' Texan

They may have a southern drawl if they're from east Texas, or a western twang if they're from west Texas. They may sprinkle their conversation with Spanish phrases if they're from El Paso or the Rio Grande valley. But they certainly won't sound like the anchorman on national television news, unless, of course, they happen to be Bill Moyers, Walter Cronkite or Dan Rather, who just happen to be Texans.

The first thing you need to understand about people who grew up in Texas is that they have been taught to say "ma'am" or "sir" from the time they were babes, and they'll probably still say "ma'am" or "sir" when they are fifty years old if you are older than they are, or if they don't know you well.

With all the people moving to Texas, the talk is becoming more standardized, especially in the big cities. But there are still a lot of pure Texan expressions around to add color to the conversation. Here are a few common ones, with Yankee translations in parentheses:

"I was just fixin' to do that." (I was thinking about doing that sometime soon.)

"Gimme a holler." (Get in touch with me.)

"God willin' and the creek don't rise." (If nothing unforeseen happens.)

"I'll be talkin' at you." (I'll speak with you soon.)

"We've howdied but we ain't shook yet." (We have spoken but have not been formally introduced.)

"Choppin' in tall cotton." (Living well.)

"He's got a burr under his saddle." (He is irritable.)

"He really chaps my hide." (He irritates me.)

"He stomped all over me." (He really let me have it.)

"You just gave it a lick and a promise." (You didn't do it well.)

"He's plumb loco." (He's crazy.)

A shirt-tailed or shoestring relative. (A distant relative, such as a second cousin twice removed.)

Chunking rocks. (Kids in Texas do not throw rocks; they chunk rocks.)

"I'll russle up a bite." (I'll prepare something to eat.)

"He's all foam and no beer." (Not worth much.)

"Taint worth diddley squat." (It isn't worth anything.)

"Slap dab in the middle." (Precisely in the middle.)

"Big hat, no cattle." (Nothing to back up his boasts.)

"Come a blue norther." (When it turns cold suddenly, especially when the temperature drop comes with a dark blue-gray sky.)

"A real gully-washer." (When it rains so fiercely that the creeks and rivers flood.)

"I've got a hankerin' for . . . " (I have a craving for . . .)

"The deal is all but saucered and blowed." (As in a cup of coffee, poured but not yet ready to drink; the deal is all but final.)

"We don't much cotton to that." (We don't like it.)

"He blew in with the tumbleweeds." (He came unexpectedly.)

"Quicker 'n scat." (Very fast.)

"He's the kind of man you'd go to the well with." (He's trustworthy.)

"I'd be on it like a duck on a junebug." (I'm eager to do something.)

"The boy's about as sharp as a marble." (He's dumb.)

"He couldn't pour spit out of a boot if the instructions were written on the heel." (He's really dumb.)

"He's about half a bubble off level." (He's a little crazy. Alternate: "He's about a brick shy of a full load," or "He's only got one oar in the water.")

"He must be from New York." (He's _really_ crazy.)

Practice

To talk good Texan, that is, with a convincing accent, one must either practice a lot or not at all. Those who choose not to practice might consider achieving an accent through artificial means: talking with a toothpick clenched between the back molars, or with a large pinch of Skoal centered behind the bottom lip.

Try to use "y'all" a lot, but remember, y'all is plural.

There is a cadence to Texas speech that makes it unique. Try reading these passages, translated from English:

Frey-ends, Ro-mins 'n cuntra min, lay-end may yore ee-yers.

Foe-ur scoe-wer 'n siven yeers ago, are foe-ur daddies brung fortha pon theis continint a nyew nayshun, dida kated tuh th' prop-o-zishun thayt awl min ur cree-yated ee-kwul.

You'll Never Get Bored
With Texas Weather

Texas weather is an exercise in extremes.

No generalities can be used because of the size of the state and the diversity of its climate. West Texas has areas that are among the driest in the nation, and parts of East Texas are among the wettest.

In the summer, the heat in south and west Texas is intense until the sun goes down, and it has been said that in the winter there is nothing between Amarillo and the North Pole but a barbed wire fence -- and two strands of that are down. As the saying goes, "Only damn fools and Yankees try to predict the weather in Texas."

In Texas, a blizzard can rage across the Panhandle at the same time the Rio Grande Valley is enjoying a balmy 85 degrees.

You can have a sandstorm in West Texas, a tropical depression over the Gulf Coast, and a soft, gentle, 75-degree breeze caressing the Hill Country simultaneously.

A "blue norther" can drop the temperature 50 degrees in a couple of hours.

Hurricanes periodically ravage the Gulf Coast, and a swath of west-central Texas is known as Tornado Alley.

The wind sometimes stacks tumbleweeds eight feet high along fences and buildings in West Texas.

Creeks and rivers flood their banks within minutes when a real gully-washer hits, and then within a few weeks it can become so dry that the bushes start whistling at the dogs.

Yes, there are times the weather can be a test of one's endurance. However, most of the time the weather is good. When winter comes to the Midwest, thousands of Winter Texans head for the Rio Grande valley, where the winter climate rivals that of Florida and Arizona. Since the invention of air conditioning, the population of Texas has doubled as northerners seek a new home in the Sunbelt.

How Texans feel about Texas weather is shown by the results of one survey, which asked them what they liked best and least about the state. Weather was No. 1 on both lists.

Larger Than Life Texans

It took a lot of grit to be an early Texan, and some of those strong men and women set a pattern that continues to show up in the character of present-day Texans. Our state still has more than its share of tough, bold risk-takers.

David "Davy" Crockett

Davy Crockett lived in Texas less than six months before his death at the Alamo established him forever as a Texan. His reputation as a bear-hunter, Indian fighter and man of rare common sense led to his election to Congress from Tennessee. It was said he was always ready with a story, usually one with an element of exaggeration, an ability much admired by Texans. His independence was too much for the political powers of Tennessee, and he found himself defeated for re-election. Smarting from the rejection, he informed his constituents: "You all can go to Hell, I'm a-goin to Texas."

Davy arrived in Texas in 1835 to start a new life. He was in Nacogdoches when he heard about the conflict with President Antonio López de Santa Anna of Mexico, and he and the dozen Tennessee Mounted Volunteers traveling with him left immediately for San Antonio.

When he arrived at the garrison he told Colonel William Barret Travis, Jim Bowie, James Bonham and the other men already gathered there: "I have come to aid you all that I can in your noble cause."

He gave his life for Texas on March 6, 1836, as did some 185 others who chose death over surrender.

Commander of the Alamo -
Bejar, Feby. 24th, 1836 -

To the People of Texas & to all Americans in the World -
Fellow citizens & compatriots -

I am besieged, by a thousand or more of the Mexicans under Santa Anna - I have sustained continuous Bombardment & cannonade for 24 hours & have not lost a man - The enemy has demanded a surrender at discretion, otherwise, the garrison are to be put to the sword, if the fort is taken - I have answered the demand with a cannon shot, & our flag still waves proudly from the walls - <u>I shall never surrender or retreat.</u> Then, I call on you in the name of Liberty, of patriotism & everything dear to the American character, to come to our aid, with all dispatch - The enemy is receiving reinforcements daily & will no doubt increase to three or four thousand in four or five days. If this call is neglected, I am determined to sustain myself as long as possible & die like a soldier who never forgets what is due to his own honor & that of his own country - <u>Victory or Death.</u>

WILLIAM BARRET TRAVIS
Lt. Col. Comdt.

Stephen F. Austin

Stephen F. Austin earned the title "Father of Texas" by opening the frontier to colonization when it was still unknown Mexican territory. He was smart, educated, and blessed with the ability to envision what the land could become. Austin set standards for those invited to be a part of his colony: "No frontiersman who has no other occupation than that of hunter will be received -- no drunkard, no gambler, no profane swearer, no idler." The thousand-plus families of "good character" he brought to Texas helped to stabilize the wild frontier.

Sam Houston

    Sam Houston was a complicated, controversial giant of a man whose personality and idiosyncrasies are legendary. He was the hero who led the ragtag volunteer Texas army to victory at the Battle of San Jacinto. Elected as the first president of the Republic of Texas, later as U. S. senator and finally as governor, he dominated the first thirty years of Texas history.

His vigorous political leadership led to the annexation of the Republic of Texas by the United States. Then, when the furor arose over the secession of Texas from the Union, he took the unpopular and losing stand. It was his refusal to take the oath of allegiance to the Confederacy that ended his political career, causing the secessionists in the state legislature to throw him out of office. Saddened, Sam Houston died two years later in 1863.

José Antonio Navarro

José Antonio Navarro was the only Texas-born man in the assembly that wrote the Texas Constitution. He was born in San Antonio in 1795, of Spanish descent. A man of great ability, Navarro was elected to several positions in the Mexican government, where he worked to colonize Texas.

Unable to accept the dictates of President Santa Anna, he took a stand in 1835 on the side of independence for Texas. He was arrested and thrown into the foulest dungeon in Mexico City, where Santa Anna condemned him to death. A court overruled the death sentence and Navarro later escaped to Texas, where he received a hero's welcome. He was an advocate of Texas statehood and later became the only Mexican delegate to the convention of 1845 in which it was decided that the Republic of Texas would join the Union.

Cynthia Ann Parker

Cynthia Ann Parker was kidnapped by the Comanches when she was nine years old and lived with them until she was recaptured by frontier soldiers at age 34. The soldiers noticed her light hair and eyes, guessed her identity and brought her and her young daughter, Topsannah, back to her white family. Cynthia Ann had totally accepted the Comanche way of life and was miserable in the white world. She had been married to Chief Peta Nacona and had borne him two sons, Pecos and Quanah, as well as Topsannah. Her white family kept her prisoner to prevent her from escaping back to her tribe. Topsannah fell ill and died, driving Cynthia Ann mad. She mourned by tearing out her hair, scarifying her breasts and, finally, starving herself to death.

Her son Quanah became one of the last warrior Comanche chiefs and represented the Indian nations at treaty meetings in Washington. His hostility toward whites was intense, undoubtedly inflamed by his mother's tragedy as well as treaty betrayals.

Jane Long

Jane Long was one of the earliest white women to settle permanently in Texas. Her courage, determination and the belief that she was the mother of the first white child born in Texas earned her the title "mother of Texas." Her husband left her and their six-year-old daughter at a small fort near Galveston while he journeyed to Mexico. When the soldiers and other settlers vacated the fort, Jane, who was pregnant, elected to stay behind with her daughter and a 12-year-old servant girl, Kian, to wait for her husband. It was an unusually bitter winter and they survived on fish and oysters dug from the frozen beach. In December, Jane, assisted by Kian, gave birth. A few days later they looked across the bay and saw several Karankawa Indian war canoes approaching. Jane hoisted her red petticoat on the flagpole and fired the fort's cannon until the Karankawas turned back. She later played a role in early Texas history by running a boarding house that was a gathering place for many who were involved in the fight for Texas independence. She died in 1880 at the age of 82.

Henrietta King

Henrietta King, "la patrona" of the most famous ranch in Texas, started her marriage to steamboat Captain Richard King in a small *jacal*, or adobe hut. Sixty years later she owned a ranch so big -- 600,000 acres -- that a man on horseback needed a full week of steady riding to make a complete circuit of its outer fence. She amassed one of the largest fortunes of any woman in America.

She raised five children while dealing with marauding Indians, assorted bandits, horse and cattle thieves, Yankee soldiers and other reprobates in an area called the Wild Horse Desert. She was described as "so resolute" that outlaws and drifters in the area claimed they would "rather tangle with the Captain than with Henrietta."

At the same time, her hospitality was such that the King Ranch became famous throughout the country. She entertained the poor and the rich, the humble and the famous, including Robert E. Lee, a close friend of the Captain. General Lee even helped them choose the site of the large hacienda. She was also called "Little Mother of Kingsville," due to her concern for hundreds of ranch workers. Henrietta added graciousness and a touch of civilization to the wild, untamed South Texas area. She died in 1925 at the age of 93.

Favorite Texas Pastimes

Going to football games: grade school, junior high, high school, college, university, professional, or backyard.

Hunting anything that's legal: dove, quail, wild turkey, deer, javelina.

Telling Aggie jokes. (Or, if you happen to be an Aggie, telling jokes about the tea-sips in Austin.)

Going to the rodeo.

Wearing cowboy boots and old bluejeans.

Two-stepping around a sawdust-floored honkytonk
to your favorite country band.

Driving around back roads to see the hills covered
with bright spring bluebonnets.

Pitching horseshoes.   Playing golf in January.

Eating, dancing and drinking beer at
one of the state's many Oktoberfests.

Listening to live music: country, western,
rock, jazz, cajun, blues, conjunto or
classical. They all flourish because
a Texan's appetite for music is so big.

Wind-surfing on Corpus Christi Bay
or on a big Texas lake.

Sand-surfing on the dunes of Sandhills State
Park near Monahans in west Texas.

Tubing down the river with a spare tube
attached just to hold the cooler of longnecks.

Taking part in a chili cook-off by
helping a friend who has
a great new chili recipe.

Watching the world's biggest
sunsets from the back porch
of a ranch house, or from the
penthouse of a skyscraper.

Finding a great barbecue joint
that no one else has discovered. . .
yet.

Searching for the perfect
margarita.

Being grateful New York City and
Los Angeles are where they are.

Celebrating the Fourth of July
at a Willie Nelson picnic, even
if Willie can't make it.

Telling our visitors
"Don't mess
with Texas."

Talkin'
Texan.

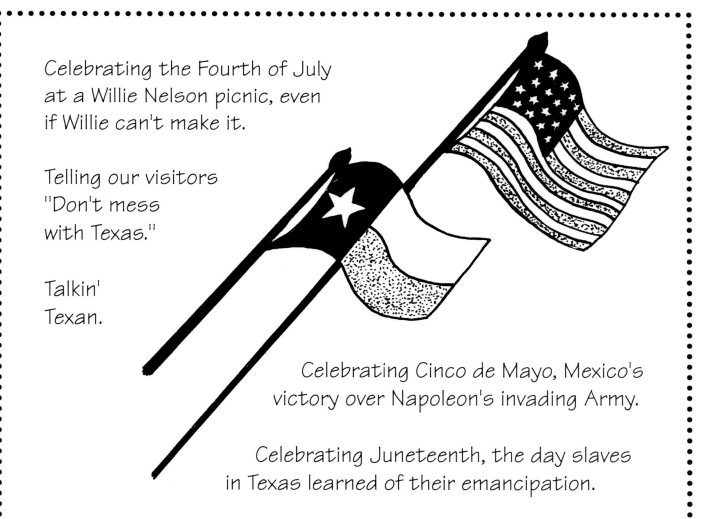

Celebrating Cinco de Mayo, Mexico's
victory over Napoleon's invading Army.

Celebrating Juneteenth, the day slaves
in Texas learned of their emancipation.

And, of course, remembering the Alamo.

Texas protects its environment, and Texans are serious about the anti-pollution message of "Don't Mess With Texas." When she was First Lady, as part of her "Keep America Beautiful" campaign, Lady Bird Johnson raised the awareness of Texans to their natural heritage.

In addition to its many parks and recreation areas, Texas has 10 national wildlife refuges where visitors can enjoy unspoiled coastal areas and bird sanctuaries. Some of the rare species that call Texas home are the whooping crane, the ocelot, the jaguarundi and the American alligator.

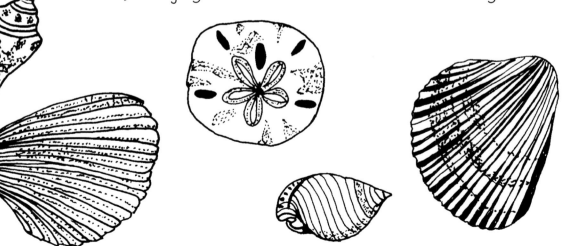

Legends of Texas
The Legend of the White Buffalo

Before the white man came, millions of buffalo roamed the prairies of North America, many of them in the land that would become Texas. Some herds were so large, observers said, that they stretched miles across and took several days to pass an observation point. But the white man slaughtered the buffalo for their hides, until only a few of the great animals were left.

According to Kiowa legend, a Great White Buffalo will return some day to lead a giant herd out of a cave in the Panhandle, and Indians will once again have their lands back.

The Legend of the Bluebonnets

Once upon a time, the land that would become Texas was plagued by a terrible drought. The Indian tribe had danced their rain dances many times in futile attempts to bring the rain. Finally, in desperation, the elders of the tribe decided that they had to make a sacrifice of their most precious possession to the Great Spirit.

As the elders debated into the night about which possession to choose, a little orphan girl listened carefully. She knew without question that her most precious possession was her buckskin doll, with a beautiful headdress of feathers from a jay, made by her mother shortly before her death.

Late that night, after everyone else was asleep, the little girl crept from her tipi to the council fire, where a few embers still glowed. Her tears fell as she placed her beloved doll on the few remaining coals and blew on the embers until fire consumed her sacrifice.

When she awoke the next morning, the hills around her village were blanketed with flowers the same azure color as the feathers in the headdress of her precious doll. Soon a gentle rain began to fall, and the terrible drought ended. Each spring since that time, the beautiful bluebonnets return to cover the hills and valleys of Texas.

The Legend of Pecos Bill

Pecos Bill is the role model for Texas cowpunchers, the Paul Bunyon of Texas. He was raised by a family of coyotes, which explains why he could run so fast that when he was in a really big hurry, he'd jump off his horse, Widowmaker, and use his own two legs.

Pecos Bill threw the loop of his lariat around an entire herd of cattle when they began to get nervous and had a mind to stampede. Once he managed to lasso a bolt of lightning before it could cause any damage.

When the cowboys he worked with faced the big job of fencing the entire ranch, he managed to talk his friends the prairie dogs into digging the post holes. He made a mark with his boot heel wherever a hole was needed, pounded the fence post into the hole behind the prairie dogs, and let the rest of the cowboys string the barbed wire.

Standing on the banks of the Rio Grande, Pecos Bill once saw a beautiful girl riding an enormous catfish. She was Slue-foot Sue, who became the love of his life and shared in many of his adventures.

Pecos Bill's last and most famous exploit was roping a Texas tornado, jumping on it and riding it all the way to Arizona. A terrible struggle followed, and the Grand Canyon was gouged from the earth as the cyclone bucked and kicked to get rid of Bill.

With the last of its strength, the tornado threw Pecos Bill so high into the sky that he still hasn't come back down.

And that's the truth.

The Legend of the Easter Fires

On Easter Eve more than a century ago, the fires of the Indians camping on hillsides near Fredericksburg frightened the children of the early German settlers. A quick-thinking mother calmed the children by telling them that the fires were built by Easter bunnies to boil the eggs they would be delivering the next morning. This story was so loved by the children that, each Easter eve, the men of Fredericksburg, dressed as Indians, build fires in the hills, and women and children, dressed as settlers, re-enact the legend.

Spanish Moss

The enormous oaks in the bayous of east Texas are adorned with garlands of gray Spanish moss. In an old Indian legend, the North Wind and the South Wind were jealous of the territory ruled by the other. This led to a fierce battle between the two giants that lasted several days. The battle ended when the South Wind tore the beard from the face of the North Wind, scattering it far and wide. The remnants of the beard caught in the trees all over the South, a reminder that the South Wind rules wherever Spanish moss is found.

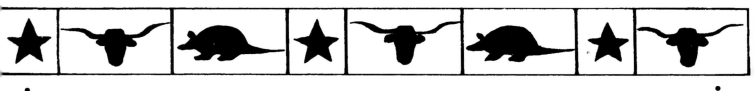

It Helps If You're
A Little Loco

Crazy things have been going on in Texas since people started coming here. In 1896, in the countryside outside Waco, the Missouri, Kansas and Texas Railroad staged a publicity stunt that featured a head-on collision of two locomotives going full speed. Thousands of people came from all over the country to watch. When the trains met, steam and pieces of metal from the crash flew in every direction, killing two spectators and injuring dozens more.

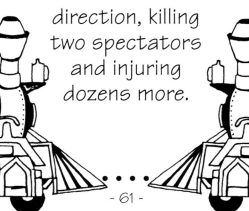

How about coming to the town of Sweetwater next spring for the annual Sweetwater Rattlesnake Roundup? Ninety-eight percent of all snakebites in Texas happen at this kind of sporting event.

A lot of Good Ol' Boys in Texas chew tobacco, and through experience they have developed their spitting skills to the highest levels. Accuracy and distance are considered attributes in spitting contests, which are among the more, uh, special events in Texas. Spectators are advised to choose their viewing locations very carefully.

Cow-chip throwing contests have not yet achieved Olympic event status, but they are considered serious athletic events at many of the festivals, county fairs and Oktoberfests around the state. No small measure of the skill is in choosing just the right cow patty. If it is too moist, it could disintegrate before it reaches the target; if it is too dry, it may lack the necessary heft to achieve the distance desired. It is a moment of high drama as the spectators watch contestants select their chips.

Every year, on the second Saturday in August, some 100,000 riders show up for the Hotter 'N' Hell Hundred bicycle ride in Wichita Falls, where they ride 100 miles in what is often 100-degree heat, just for the fun of it.

Tens of thousands of college students converge on South Padre Island for the annual Spring Break party, which goes nonstop for a month.

Each spring the Yuppies in north Austin and the Bubbas in south Austin flex their muscles in a tug-of-war, to see if the quiche-eating wine-drinkers can pull the chicken-fried steak-eating beer drinkers into the mud. South Austin always wins, but the Yuppies are too polite to give up.

Cadillac Ranch makes a flamboyant state-
ment of some kind. In a field along the side of
Interstate 40 west of Amarillo, a bunch of
Cadillacs are buried up to their windshields in
the ground with tail fins jutting toward the
afternoon sun, a formation that looks like a
giant has been playing mumblety-peg with cars.

Hollywood, Texas

The movie makers in Hollywood quickly discovered that movies about Texas made money. The first three decades of "moving pictures" saw dozens of Texas titles, including *Texas Tex, Texas Flash, Texas Tommy, Texas Terror, Texas Gunfighter, Texas Kid, Texas Trail, Texas Justice, Texas Stampede, Texas Bad Man, Texas Tornado, Man From Texas, Kid From Texas, Lady From Texas, Cowboys From Texas, Angel From Texas, Two Guys From Texas, The Pal From Texas, The Gentleman From Texas, The Stranger From Texas* . . . The three words most used in movie titles, in fact, are Love, Hell, and Texas.

Texas was a frontier state known for its cowboys, Indians, heroes and outlaws. If the movie wasn't good, the director could put in enough shooting, riding, roping and ranching to keep the Saturday matinee audiences happy. And so the myth was born that all Texans were cowboys or rangers, saloon-hall damsels or innocent schoolmarms, and that Texas was a land of sagebrush, cactus and tumbleweed.

The box-office success of the early Westerns led to an upgrading of both actors and plots. Texans became taller when Gary Cooper, John Wayne, Jimmy Stewart and Clark Gable replaced Tom Mix, Gene Autry and Roy Rogers. Such movies as *Red River, Rio Grande, Rio Lobo, The Alamo, The Searchers* and *The Wild Bunch* were still Westerns about Texas, but they were better Westerns.

With the oil boom in Texas came such oil stories as *Boom Town, Hud, Giant, Lucy Gallant, The Wheeler Dealers,* and of course the television series *Dallas*. The ranch was still part of the Texas movie, but it was the oil derrick, not cattle, that was central to the plot. A big change came in the way Texans were portrayed. Now they were often rich but their taste was garish and the wife thought nothing of flying the private plane to Neiman Marcus to spend a fortune in an afternoon. The modest Texas cattleman gave way to the bragging, wheeler dealer oilman.

Perhaps it was the Kennedy assassination in Dallas, or perhaps all the themes were exhausted, but Hollywood seemed to lose interest in Texas for several years. When Texans appeared in movies it was usually as a bragging, drawling, leering caricature.

In recent years there have been many movies filmed in Texas, but, with the exception of *The Best Little Whorehouse in Texas* or *The Texas Chainsaw Massacre*, the Texas theme is underplayed. Among the critically acclaimed films set in Texas, and in which Texas, Texans and their stories are important, are *The Last Picture Show*, *Urban Cowboy*, *Bonnie and Clyde*, *Places in the Heart*, *Terms of Endearment*, *Tender Mercies*, *The Trip to Bountiful*, *True Stories* and *Texasville*. Texas movies have come full circle with the TV mini-series Lonesome Dove. The success of this cowboy Western, featuring two crusty old Texas Rangers, has revived interest in the Old West themes.

Texas Etiquette

Most people raised in Texas are gentle and polite. They are taught "mind your manners" from infancy. Manners, in Texas, are more a matter of courtesy and respect than rules of etiquette.

A native-born Texan will always tip his hat or touch two fingers to the brim when he meets a lady on the street.

Never make fun of a Texan's hat.

Children are taught to say, "Ma'am" and "Sir" to anyone older. Example: "Billy Joe, did you bring in the dog?" Billy Joe answers "yes." "Yes what, Billy Joe?" "Yes, Sir!" This habit continues well into adulthood.

Texans always respect your right to be in a hurry, even if they aren't. A slow-moving car or truck will move over onto the shoulder of a two-lane highway to make it easier for a faster driver to pass.

Don't forget to say "thank you" by giving a little wave after you've gone on by.

It is not fit nor proper to ask a Texas rancher how big his ranch is. No matter how large it is, it is "a little spread."

Going over or under a rancher's fence without his permission is more than bad manners. It's trespassing, and property lines are not violated in Texas. It could even lead to a little buckshot in your britches. And if the buckshot doesn't get your attention, maybe those bulls will.

Texans generally don't jump right into a discussion about anything, least of all business, without first inquiring about family, health, and one's opinion of the weather. Yankees, not knowing any better, tend to get impatient after several minutes of preliminaries.

Unlike the movies, a true Texan always removes his hat when he enters a house or restaurant where ladies are present. And until proven otherwise, all women are ladies.

It is sometimes considered rude to eat barbecue with silverware, except maybe a knife. Be prepared to use your fingers, and get lots of napkins. Avoid wearing white.

And the most important act of courtesy taught to all young Texans: It is rude to ask a man where he is from.
If he's from Texas, he'll tell you.
If he isn't, don't embarrass him.

Texas Wish List

Texans wish they really were as rich as most people think they are.

Texans wish Texas would have another boom and that this time they wouldn't mess it up.

Texans wish the rest of the country would realize when they are joking and when they are being serious.

Texans wish the rest of the country would realize that Texans love the United States more (or at least as much as) they love Texas.

Texans wish that Alaska was about half the size it is.

Texans wish that those loud, obnoxious, bragging impostors would stop telling people that they are Texans.

Texans wish that people in the less fortunate 49 states would not assume that all of Texas was flat and desolate, with little vegetation except cacti and tumbleweed.

Texans wish non-Texans would quit assuming they can't speak English, and would realize that they take pride in having their own expressive state language.

Texans wish visitors realized that the "Don't Mess With Texas" slogan is aimed at keeping people from throwing trash on Texas highways and beaches.

Texans wish every child in the cities back East had the chance to walk in a field of bluebonnets, to see the sun set over the vast Texas horizon, and to camp out under the stars on a clear, Texas night.

Texans wish the revisionist writers and historians would stop telling them that their heroes were not as heroic as they believe.

Texans wish that Alabama had kept its imported fire ants all to itself.

Texans wish they could annex Colorado, but just for use in August and in ski season.

Texans wish Oklahoma would take up a sport other than football. Knitting, perhaps.

Texans wish they really did own a ranch and an oil well.

Texans wish the rest of the world did not think that J.R. Ewing and Southfork were real.

Texans wish that everyone could have as much fun in life as they do.

Texas Tastes

The time has come to put aside the stereotyped belief that Texans eat mostly barbecue, four-alarm chili, pinto beans and chicken-fried steak. Like the state itself, Texas food is extraordinarily diverse. Some Texans speak dreamily of golden-fried chicken, flaky-crusted pies, beans simmered with ham hocks, cornbread and baking-powder biscuits. Others delight in a hot plate of tacos, red beans and rice. Either way, Texas food is something special.

Barbecue is a favorite menu for a gathering of Texans. It takes a lot of time to do barbecue right -- many cooks say it takes 12 to 14 hours for the smoke to cook the meat properly, and the slower the better -- so if you get a sudden urge for barbecue you'll have to look for one of the state's many smokehouses. Luckily, almost every town has one. Or several.

Barbecue can be brisket, ribs, sausage, chicken, wild game, ham, seafood or whole animals. The meat is smoked over green oak or mesquite embers, basted now and then with a mixture of oil, vinegar or lemon juice, as well as seasonings that most chefs will refuse to divulge.

Central Texas is known as the Barbecue Belt, and on many evenings the breezes carry the rich aromas of slow-cooked meats over the countryside.

The red tomato goop that is called barbecue sauce by some people -- typically Georgians and Carolinians and others who simply don't know any better -- is not used when cooking true Texas barbecue.

Chili is the official state dish, and it is made with whatever meat is available. Chili is simmered long and slow, with a few special ingredients in just the right portions to give it some character. Arguments over what goes into the pot to make the best "bowl of red" are as hot as the chili itself. You can count on two things: The chili will be hot, and it will have no beans. If it has beans, it is called "gringo chili." Although Texans eat a lot of chili, the hype and showmanship of many Texas chili contests are mostly for fun, and have little to do with the chili that the contestants cook for themselves.

At least, we don't *think* they really put fire ants in their recipes at home . . .

Chicken-fried steak is ordered by more people in more restaurants and cafes in Texas than any other dish on the menu. This batter-fried, tenderized steak smothered in rich cream gravy is a sure way to light a Texas man's fire.

Tex-Mex has been called the Texification of Mexican cooking. It started in San Antonio. Mexican women wrapped spicy meat in a tortilla to sell to trail drivers and ranchers, who welcomed the change from their regular diet of coffee, beans and biscuits. People who aren't familiar with Tex-Mex cooking think it's hot, but most of it is not. The salsas, picante sauce and *pico de gallo* that are served with the tacos, enchiladas, burritos and fajitas can vary in firepower and can be adjusted to your level of tolerance.

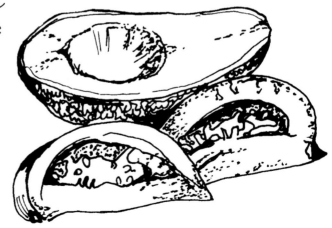

With 500 miles of Gulf Coast, Texas has a bounty of fresh shrimp, oysters and fish. Naturally, seafood is popular throughout the Lone Star State. And we can't forget all those catfish and bass that Texas fishermen bring home to be fried with some hushpuppies and sliced okra.

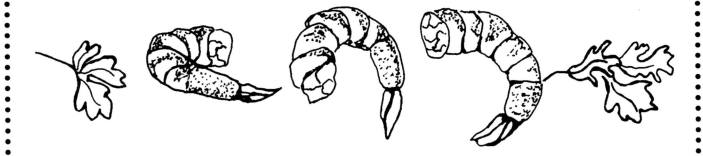

Immigrants from every corner of the world have settled in Texas, and they've brought their distinctive cooking styles with them. Mexican, French, Chinese, Southern . . . it's all here.

Central Texas attracted large colonies of Germans famous for their sausage-making skills, and Oktoberfests draw big crowds of beer-drinking, wurst-eating Texans.

If Texans were polled on their favorite drink, the odds are that iced tea would be the easy winner. Great big glasses of *real tea* are offered by friends or restaurants the minute you walk in the door. Beer in longneck bottles or cans, Dr Pepper (there's a Dr Pepper museum in Waco!) and margaritas (frozen or on the rocks, with salt) are consumed in large quantities. And Texas wines are also beginning to receive international acclaim. Regions of west Texas are said to have soil and climate conditions equal to the great wine regions of Europe and California. If you're headed for a picnic, a bottle of Texas white wine can go right into the cooler with the beer.

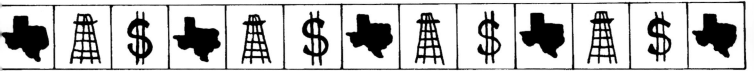

Texas Types

Good Ol' Boys

Good ol' boys can be counted on to act Texan, think Texan and talk Texan. They show up for coffee most mornings at the town cafe, where they trade observations about the weather, politics, the high school football team, and either the next or the last hunting trip they were on. They think a lot of their hunting dogs, kids and wives, frequently in that order.

You can identify them by the bumper sticker:

> **MY DAUGHTER & MY MONEY**
> **GO TO**
> **TEXAS TECH**

The Texas Exes

Their spiritual home is Austin, and many of them never left after college. They love it when the U.T. Tower glows orange, and consider football season the best time of year (as long as the Longhorns are winning).

Look for the bumper sticker on the Mercedes:

Texas Ex

Aggies

Aggies are necessary to Texas so that all the ethnic jokes from other places can be translated into Aggie jokes. They are fiercely loyal to the Texas A&M tradition and have trouble finding anything nice to say about the tea-sips in Austin. They buy their airplanes, cars, trucks, tractors and clothes in Aggie maroon and white. They are generally good-natured about the ribbing they get for being hayseeds, probably because A&M has attracted more National Merit Scholars than most universities in the country, along with an impressive number of Rhodes scholars and Nobel Prize winners.

Look for the bumper sticker on the Cadillac:

HONK If I'm an AGGIE

Kickers

During the day they may drive a truck or work behind a desk or counter, but at night they are decked out in cowboy boots and fancy hat, drinking beer and two-stepping around the floor of some honkytonk. They wear big belt buckles, and usually have their names carved into their belts, which comes in handy if they need help finding their way home.

Longnecks & Longhorns
No Place But Texas

Bubbas

Bubbas are essentially kickers who have slightly more difficulty holding steady jobs. They are commonly sighted cruising around in a beat-up pickup truck with a rifle or fishing pole in the gun rack. In the truck bed, one often finds a 40-pound sack of dog food and at least a 12-pack's worth of empty beer cans. Belt buckles are smaller and bellies are bigger than kicker's. Gimme caps are preferred headgear. Bubbas _love_ a good ruckus.

The bumper of the pickup is practically held on by bumper stickers, of which some of the most popular are:

> **TOUCH MY TRUCK
> AND YOU DIE**

> **Texas Crude**

Snowbirds

Also known as Winter Texans. They come primarily from the Midwest and congregate in the Rio Grande valley from November to May. Most of them arrive in big RV's and campers, find a good parking space, and spend the next few months playing shuffleboard and pitching horseshoes. They are welcome visitors to the Valley, much loved by local merchants. Not to be confused with Spring Breakers who flock to the same areas in February and March.

Somewhere near the personalized license plate, look for the following bumper sticker:

```
I'm Spending My
Children's Inheritance
```

Retired Military

They gather around Texas's many military bases, especially ones with a good PX and a hospital. The American flag flies on a properly lighted flagpole every day that it doesn't rain. Always found at Fourth of July parades and Republican picnics. They've been around, and you can learn a lot from them about what's really happening in the world.

Rarely display bumper sentiments, with the possible exception of a Republican campaign sticker and:

Support Your Troops

Oilmen

Although Texas is famous for them, they are an endangered species. Oil has become big business and the corporations are now the ones who own the leases and make the deals. As for the independent oilmen who are left, their state of mind and the desire to drill new wells is directly related the the price of a barrel of Texas crude. They can occasionally be sighted in Midland-Odessa, Houston, or East Texas at the Petroleum Club. They are gamblers, willing to win big or lose it all, and if they have been around long they have probably done both several times over.

Texas still has a lot of people who earn their living in the oil patch, including geologists, engineers, computer specialists, and the executives and workers who make the oil companies run, but the heart-stopping thrill of bringing in the Big One with only a handful of men is gone.

They've learned enough not to drive fancy cars, even when the price of crude is in an up cycle. You may see an clean pickup with the following sticker:

DEAR LORD PLEASE
SEND ANOTHER OIL BOOM
& I PROMISE NOT TO
MESS IT UP THIS TIME

Naturalized Texans

Some of these transplants from other states came willingly, others came by company transfer, but a surprising number put down roots and say, "This is where I want to be." Like most converts, they soon out-Texan the native Texans. They get a pair of cowboy boots, learn the Cotton-Eyed Joe, practice saying "y'all," and embark on a serious effort to identify the better barbecue joints in town. Pretty soon they're calling friends back home to gloat about the winter weather.

   The prouder ones sport such stickers as:

I wasn't born in   **TEXAS**   **but I got here as quick as I could**

NATURALIZED   TEXAN

Native Texans

   Last but certainly not least. They are born with the inalienable right to call themselves Texans no matter if cruel fate has taken them beyond the loving borders of their fair state. They know they are different, and can't imagine what it would be like not to be Texan. They are naturally friendly and polite, and are delighted to live up to the role of "being Texan" when entertaining visitors or traveling. They are proud of their heroes. They are a little puzzled by all the stereotyped images they see called Texans in the movies and on television.

Native Texans love bumper stickers. Following are some of our favorites:

NATIVE TEXAN

American By Birth
Texan By The Grace Of God

101% TEXAN

Don't Mess With
Texas

I BLEED ORANGE

COWBOY CADILLAC

TEXAS SECEDE!

LET'S RODEO

Texans
Talk Friendly

Ropers
Aren't Dopers

On Earth As It Is In
Texas

I BRAKE FOR
ARMADILLOS
& HALLUCINATIONS

Onward Through the Fog

Keep Texas Safe
Arm A Dillo

Republic of TEXAS

IF I'M GOOD & SAY MY PRAYERS
WHEN I DIE I'LL GO TO
TEXAS

Foat Wuth,
Ah Luv Yew

There are two kinds of people:
__TEXANS__ and those who
wish they were

Life's Too Short
Not To Live It As A Texan

There's Magic in Texas ...

. . . When spring arrives and the bluebonnets and Indian paintbrush cover miles and miles of the roadsides and hills of central, south and east Texas.

. . . When you walk at night under the west Texas sky, with stars so bright you feel they reach down and touch you.

. . . When a good rain falls in the desert regions of Big Bend country, followed by a profusion of wildflowers, of every color and size, springing from the seemingly barren land.

. . When evening falls and the luminarias are lit to form a necklace of soft lights across the arching bridges and along the Riverwalk during Christmas season in San Antonio.

. . . When Marshall, in East Texas, turns on 3 million tiny white lights, transforming the entire town into a holiday fantasy.

. . . When the trees, shrubs and grass are decorated with thousands of monarch butterflies as they make an overnight stop in the Highland Lakes region on their annual migration to Central America.

. . . When the sunset in Austin is followed by a moment when the western sky is illuminated by a flash of lavender, giving the capital its nickname, "City of the Violet Crown."

. . . When at dusk the deer take their new fawns to explore the Hill Country.

. . . When the Marfa lights, a mystery since they were first called "ghost lights" by cowboys on cattle drives in the 1880's, flicker in the dark near the south Texas town.

... When sunsets borrow the colors of the wildflowers..

... When a dark, rumbling thunderstorm rolls across the plains, followed by golden rays of sunlight.

... When the mockingbird gives his twilight serenade.

... When friends and family come to visit for the holidays, or any time at all.

. . . When a full moon shines on the Enchanted Rock near Johnson City, a mountain-size, pink granite dome. The mica glistening in the moonlight and the sounds the rock makes as it contracts from the night's chill help you understand why the Indians considered it a sacred place.

. . . When you walk through the museum at the Alamo and become aware of the dozens of people quietly sharing this moment with you, hushed in reverence for the courage this shrine memorializes.

Peg Hein and Kathryn Lewis

PEG HEIN , a fourth-generation Texan, spent her early years in Texas before moving to the Midwest. It was those years away from her home state that made her realize how special and unique a place Texas is. She is the author of several best-selling cookbooks, including *Tastes & Tales From Texas . . . With Love*, and *MORE Tastes and Tales From Texas*. Peg lives with her husband in the Texas Hill Country near Austin.

KATHRYN LEWIS wasn't born in Texas, but "she got here as quick as she could." With four preceding generations Texas-born and raised, the draw to the Lone Star State was irresistible. Kathryn produces and designs gift items that are sold throughout the country. "Life's Too Short Not to Live It As a Texan" is the fourth book collaboration with Peg, her mother. Kathryn lives in Austin with her husband and two children.

Kathryn
Designs

Additional copies of <u>Life's Too Short Not to Live It as a Texan</u> can be ordered for $6.95, plus $1.50 postage and handling, from **Kathryn Designs, 13 Sundown Parkway, Austin, TX 78746-5201**

Please send ___copies of <u>Life's Too Short Not to Live It as a Texan</u>
To:

Name _____

Address _____

City _____ State _____ Zip _____

Texas residents add 55 cents sales tax.